PATTY and GINGER share and TAKE TURNS

Adventures of the Fruit Clique

Lezlie Brown-Roberts

4

This book is dedicated to all the kids around the world.

Patty the pineapple and Ginger the apple were fighting over who was going to get to play with their favorite toy during break at school. They both wanted a turn but only one of them could use it at a time. They were pulling and tugging at the toy demanding that they got to be the one to get it that day. Their friends wanted to help them stop and get along again. Sometimes even good friends can fight, and it was up to the others to remind them that they liked each other and could all get along.

The first one that tried to do something was Perry the pear that wanted to show them there was a better way to do things.

"You two can figure out who gets the toy peacefully. There is no reason to both be pulling at it. What if you both let go on the count of three and then we can all talk about this. 1...2...3." Neither one let go though and Perry didn't know what else to try.

"What if one of you was just patient and waited for your turn to play with the toy. Maybe you could both get a smaller turn today instead of one of you getting it the whole time." Jill the orange suggested, but neither one wanted to give up getting to use the toy first.

This was a really hard problem and none of the friends knew what could make them stop fighting and become friends again. Geo the grapes tried to tell them that pulling on the toy might break it and they had to be gentle, or nobody would end up getting to play with it.

Kelly the Kiwi urged them to be kind to each other and should want to be the one to give up the toy to the other one.

Sonny the banana meanwhile was trying to convince them that if they just used self-control they could both calm down and wouldn't be angry about it anymore.

Meanwhile Faith the watermelon knew that something was going to work to get them back together.

Without the love though how would we all play together later?" Her words made the to stop fighting.

The last person to try talking to the friends was Linda the strawberry.

"You two are best friends and love each other. If you really did love each other than the toy wouldn't matter. After school the toy ends up staying here and the two of you get to leave and play anything you want together. friends.

They realized that all of their friends were right, and it was wrong to want to keep the toy all for themselves. They could share the toy and then both of them would be happy. In school there are only so many things to play with and it is important to make sure everyone gets a turn too. When you share with others in school it can even be a way to get new friends.

The End